Montesquieu

THE TEMPLE OF GNIDE

*Translated and with an Introduction by
Brian Stableford*

THIS IS A SNUGGLY BOOK

Translation and Introduction Copyright © 2022
by Brian Stableford.
All rights reserved.

ISBN: 978-1-64525-096-8

Charles-Louis de Secondat, Baron de La Brède et de Montesquieu (1689-1755), generally referred to simply as Montesquieu, was a French judge, political philosopher and man of letters of the Enlightenment. In 1721 he anonymously published *Lettres persanes*, which satirized French Regency society, as seen by fictitious Persians. He later devoted himself to his great works which combined history and political philosophy: *Considérations sur les causes de la grandeur des Romains et de leur décadence* (1734) and *De l'Esprit des lois* (1748), in which he developed his ideas on the distribution of the functions of the State between its different components, later called the "principle of separation of powers." Montesquieu, along with John Locke among others, is one of the thinkers of the political and social organization on which modern and politically liberal societies are based.

Brian Stableford's scholarly work includes *New Atlantis: A Narrative History of Scientific Romance* (Wildside Press, 2016), *The Plurality of Imaginary Worlds: The Evolution of French roman scientifique* (Black Coat Press, 2017) and *Tales of Enchantment and Disenchantment: A History of Faerie* (Black Coat Press, 2019). He has translated more than three hundred volumes from the French, mostly in the genres of *roman scientifique, contes de fées* and Romantic and Symbolist fiction. His recent fiction includes the visionary science fiction novel *The Revelations of Time and Space* (2020) and its sequel *After the Revelation* (2021); the last in his long series of "Tales of the Genetic Revolution," *The Elusive Shadows* (2020); and the comedy fantasy *Meat on the Bone* (2021), all published by Snuggly Books.

CONTENTS

INTRODUCTION

LE TEMPLE DE GNIDE was published anonymously in 1725, in an edition whose title page claimed—falsely—that it had been published in London. The true place of its publication was Paris. 1725 was during the early years of the reign of Louis XV, not long after the end of the official Regency of Philippe d'Orléans that had followed the death of Louis XV, when the boy king was deemed to have attained his majority and became the absolute monarch of France—in theory, that is. It was not uncommon at the time for books to be published in Paris with deceptive title pages claiming publication elsewhere, because the monarch had a notional monopoly on licit publication, and a royal warrant was required for books to be printed by sanctioned presses and sold in authorized bookshops. A company of royally-appointed censors was in charge of excluding from publication works that were deemed to be in some way offensive to the monarchy or the Catholic Church. By 1725, however, a massive commerce had developed in works unlicensed by the censors, the authors and printers of which were obscured or disguised in order to evade the possibility of prosecution. Copies were routinely sold by the same booksellers who sold officially-approved texts, but they were sold, as the popular phrase had it, "under the counter," without evident advertisement.

Practical considerations dictated that it was impossible actively to pursue and prosecute all unlicensed titles, so the authorities limited their attention to those considered the most offensive and turned a blind eye to the rest, although active pursuit always remained an option for the authorities if a text attracted attention for any reason, and the level of risk run by outlaw texts thus varied considerably. That circumstance was familiar to authors and publishers alike, and the caution manifest in the representation of texts also extended to their nature. Writers routinely disguised material of a potentially-contentious nature by means of various strategies of misrepresentation that gave them a gloss of respectability, or at least of harmlessness. Thus, *Le Temple de Gnide* represents itself falsely as a translation of an ancient Greek text recently rediscovered and translated for the sake of scholarly interest. It is framed in such a way as superficially to resemble a number of actual ancient Greek or Roman texts (or, at least, texts believed to be authentic) in which subject-matter that would have seemed suspect in a contemporary text— especially paganism and erotic material—was excused by its antiquity.

Robert Darnton's perceptive and thorough analysis of *The Forbidden Bestsellers of Prerevolutionary France* (1989) explains how illicit texts came to be lumped together under the label of "philosophical books," the phrase being a convenient shorthand for customers entering bookshops who wanted to know what was available "under the counter." The label covered books that the censors had outlawed because they were deemed to be politically subversive or theologically contentious and books considered to be what modern terminology describes as "pornographic"—a term originated by one of those outlaw texts, Nicolas Restif de la Bretonne's *Le Pornographe* [A Treatise on Prostitution] (1769) but somewhat perverted by the conventions of modern usage. The reason why all such texts warranted description as "philosophical" is because they questioned, explicitly or tacitly, matters that censors considered unquestionable—and hence unmentionable—ostensibly because they had been settled, once and for all, by Holy Writ, or, rather, the Roman Catholic Church's interpretation of Holy Writ.

In 1725 France was in an early phase of what came to be called the Age of Enlightenment, following on naturally from the previous century's Age of Reason. Collectively those two eras constituted a kind of Golden Age of modern philosophy, when all the crucial question of how human beings ought to live and how societies might best be organized, first raised and extensively debated in ancient Greece, were re-raised, and made considerable progress in spite of that progress being hampered and hobbled by the Church, which considered that it already had the answers to all the relevant questions, both material and moral. It was not difficult for the newly Enlightened philosophers to prove that the Church's opinions on many material questions were not only wrong but utterly absurd, although the inevitable reaction of the Church to that contention was to defend its favorite absurdities fiercely—with fire and the sword when that was practicable, and by subtler means of persuasion when it was not—but moral questions, being inherently immune to empirical testing, were more resistant to attack. The social organization and discipline of the sexual impulse—a matter of intimate interest to most adults—became the most contentious personal issue, the bedrock of the very idea of the "unmentionable" and, in common parlance, the idea of the "immoral." The reason why *Le Temple de Gnide* was, in 1725, an essentially contentious text, which had to be disguised at every level in the attempt to evade active persecution, is that it was an attempt to explore the psychological operation of the sexual impulse, and to raise the question of how the social management of that impulse might best be organized. It does that in a tortuously roundabout fashion, because there was no other way, in practical terms, for it to be done in print in France in 1725—and even so, it sailed precariously close to the wind in the context of its publication.

The author of *Le Temple de Gnide* was Charles-Louis Secondat, Baron de La Brède et de Montesquieu, who preferred to sign himself simply, after the aristocratic fashion of the day, "Montesquieu"—not that he was able to use that signature on his published works, which were all unsanctioned by the royal censors and placed on the *Index Prohibitorum* by the Church, making it a sin to read them, or even to know of their existence. Two of those works, however, *Considerations sur les causes et de la grandeur des Romains et de leur décadence* [Considerations of the causes of the Greatness of the Romans and their decline] (1734) and *De l'esprit des lois* [On the Intelligence of Laws] (1748)[1] are nowadays regarded as two of the great classics of the Enlightenment and they have had an enormous influence on modern thinking, especially via the latter's influence on the drafting of the American Constitution, one of the most evident examples of modern Holy Writ. Of all the authors of "philosophical books," Montesquieu is the one whose ideas are most greatly esteemed nowadays in Western political philosophy.

Le Temple de Gnide is a work of much lesser importance, and it is considerably more gnomic than its more frankly-argued successors,

---

1 The title is usually translated as *The Spirit of Laws*, but the French term *esprit* is considerably broader in its reference than its English transcription, and it is arguable that "intelligence" corresponds more closely than "spirit" to Montesquieu's intended meaning.

but it is nevertheless interesting and worthy of attention, at least in terms of its evasive narrative strategy. The philosophical questions it addresses cannot be considered to have been "solved" by any subsequent consensus, even to the limited degree represented in political culture by the summary slogan of *liberté, egalité, fraternité,* and the difficulty of their practical solution remains as relevant to contemporary erotic experience as it was in 1725. Precisely for that reason, those issues have been addressed, tacitly or explicitly, by vast numbers of texts written during the last two centuries, employing many different narrative strategies. Thus, *Le Temple de Gnide* can easily seem primitive and naïve by comparison with later works, but the endeavor can still be appreciated as a significant precursor of modern texts dealing with *"gnide"*—which are numbered in millions, and account for a significant proportion of all published texts, especially in the realm of fiction.

The word *gnide* was esoteric even in 1725, and has virtually vanished from usage today, but it existed in Old English as well as Old

French. It refers to the act of squeezing with the hands, and was ancestral to the modern English word "knead." The latter term is most familiar nowadays in connection with the kneading of dough in making bread, but in the context of Montesquieu's allegory *gnide* refers to the palpation of human flesh—which is to say, to the sexual embrace. The temple of Gnide is a temple of Venus,[1] dedicated to the veneration of sex in its physical expression. In its physical description of the temple of Gnide and the rites that supposedly take place there the narrative examines, in symbolic terms, the psychological operation of lust, extending from an account of the nature of sexual attraction and its usual behavioral manifestations to a consideration of the psychology of sexual jealousy with a brief aside on the effects of alcohol, symbolized by the god Bacchus and his veneration.

---

1 Montesquieu follows contemporary convention by referring to Classical deities by their Latin names, thus referring to Venus rather than Aphrodite and Amour rather than Eros, even though Gnide is supposedly located in Greece.

The encoding in the text of various arguments by means of that Classical symbolism is undeniably awkward, and it created difficulties for readers in 1725 that are augmented for modern readers, who are far less likely to recognize immediately and to understand its references. Those difficulties were deliberately constructed, in order to create a useful "potential deniability" with reference to potential attacks leveled at the text on moral grounds. A poem supposedly written thousands of years ago, before the advent of Christ, can hardly be expected to embrace the prejudices of Christianity and thus cannot be blamed for assuming different values. Naturally, a scholarly examination of those assumptions cannot logically be considered an endorsement of those values or a suggestion that they might in some fashion be preferable to Christian prejudices. We might—and surely will—suspect that to be the case, but the evil is transplanted by the narrative strategy, if not into in the mind of the reader, at least into the mind of a distant hypothetical author.

That kind of argument, by means of which an author seeks to evade culpable responsibility for his work by representing himself as a mere translator motivated by scholarly curiosity, is saturated with hypocrisy, but that is the whole point of it. If prejudice is supported by all the rhetorical weapons at its disposal—as it invariably is—that aggression inevitably calls forth all the armaments of ingenious sarcasm in reply. That, in a nutshell, is the whole history of philosophical literature, especially the kind of fiction that acquired the label during the French Enlightenment of *contes philosophiques*—a label popularized by Montesquieu's younger contemporary Voltaire, but equally applicable to the works that Montesquieu cast in fictional form, including *Lettres Persans* [Persian Letters] (1721)—in which a scathing criticism of French society is represented as the opinions and judgments of two foreign tourists whose own hypothetical culture is an Oriental despotism that licenses polygamy—as well as *Le Temple de Gnide*.

The narrative strategy of the *Lettres Persans* was not new when Montesquieu employed it, and it was to be employed again and again by other notable *contes philosophiques* in France and elsewhere. The fundamental strategy of Le *Temple de Gnide* was not new either; literary history abounds with deceptive documents falsely attributed to more-or-less respectable sources. Those deceptions that are detected, or at least suspected, are frequently consigned to a literary limbo of "apocrypha" or "pseudo-epigraphia," while the undetected are accepted at face value, at least by credulous individuals. Few people in Paris could have been fooled into thinking that *Le Temple de Gnide* really was a recently-rediscovered ancient Greek text, nor was any serious attempt made in the preparation or publication of the document to persuade potential readers that it was. Its pretence is intentionally transparent, and that is an aspect of its convoluted rhetoric. By 1725, of course, Enlightened readers were well used to such artifices, and few readers were sufficiently gullible to take claims of authenticity made in works of fiction at face value (although the joke is still told of an English clergyman said to have hurled Lemuel Gulliver's account of his travels across the room in disgust, asserting that he did not believe a word of it.)

In spite of that lack of complete originality, however, *Le Temple de Gnide* has acquired a certain reputation for literary pioneering. Rightly or wrongly, it is frequently cited as the first significant French example of a "poem in prose," and thus a notable precursor of the oxymoronic genre of "*poèmes en prose*" popularized in the 1860s by Charles Baudelaire. That classification calls attention to a significant aspect of its literary style, which involves an inherent element of paradox as well as poetic effect; the narrative aspires to seem simultaneously antiquated and new, conspicuously obsolete but immediately pertinent, and to do so by simulating a particular tone of voice and manner of presentation. That paradoxicality and mannerism have only been enhanced by the passage of time; in order to be understood and appreciated the text required sophisticated reading in 1725, of a relatively rare variety, and in order to be understood and appreciated nowadays it requires an even rarer sophistication—but it is not necessarily a bad thing for a text to present its readers with problems and challenges, although not all readers share that opinion.

The temple of Gnide, therefore, is not only a temple of Venus but a temple of narrative invention, or at least of narrative improvisation. It is not only a symbolization of lust and its psychological and social accommodation, but a symbolization of the narrativization of the erotic, a story that is as much about story construction as it is about the substance of the story being told, and for sophisticated readers, that adds an extra dimension of depth to the narrative. Not all readers will be interested in that dimension, but some might be, and might feel that it adds further interest to the problematics of even the most superficial reading of an allegory that prefers Venus to alternative representations of hypothetical divinity.

As the Holy Writ that Montesquieu was attempting, modestly, to subvert takes care to point out, its own God is a fiercely jealous god. Being founded on fantastic fictions, Churches, in all their many varieties, tend to be intolerant of rival forms of fantastic fiction, and the hostility of the Roman Catholic Church has always been remarkable for its unremitting violence, perhaps odd in a Church whose central doctrine is supposedly one of tolerance, or even of loving one's enemies. Even slight alternatives to its doctrines have tended to be construed as hideous heresies: crimes against the unchallengeable, warranting extreme and eternal punishment far beyond the mere refusal of publication. In practical terms, however, the Church has always found the extirpation of heresy impractical, no matter how strenuous its efforts of suppression have been. There have always been loopholes in its mechanisms of suppression, by means of which rival forms of fantasy have been allowed to exist, becoming tolerable and sometimes even seeming praiseworthy. There is nothing particularly unusual, therefore, about the fact that a text like *Le Temple de Gnide* was able to exist in 1725 in spite of being technically illicit, and even to thrive in a certain measure.

There had been previous periods in French history ("the Dark Ages") when the Church's attempted stranglehold on Western European belief had been more powerful, resulting in a more effective apparent suppression of rival fantasies in the media of writing and print, but practical considerations make the absolute censorship of thought impossible, and rival fantasies always evade total suppression. In the long run, skeptical reason inevitably tends to erode doctrinaire fantasy, even when dogma is supported by fire and the sword, thus leading to eventual Enlightenment—but history instructs us, as it instructed Montesquieu, that the process of erosion is neither simple nor easy and that no matter how many battles are won, or by what means, the war is likely to go on forever. When individual prejudices fall, they tend to be replaced not by open-minded skepticism but by other, sometimes more ingenious, prejudices. Montesquieu was sharply aware of that, and that awareness helped to determine the ingenuity and convolution of his particular plans of attack on the prejudices of his own day.

The specific prejudices that *Le Temple de Gnide* tries to undermine, subtly and relatively politely, are no exception to that general rule, and there is no cause for surprise in the fact that the problems the narrative identifies in the psychological and social functioning of the erotic impulse remain as acute today, everywhere in the world, as they were in France in 1725—and, for that matter, in ancient Greece three thousand years earlier. Insofar as the story suggests the direction in which solutions might be sought, it argues that the relaxation of particular sexual prejudices might have a mollifying effect: that greater tolerance and greater freedom of individual action might make life easier and more pleasant, although he did not imagine that such tolerance and liberation would be easy of achievement. That was the general direction of all of Montesquieu's philosophy, refined and generalized in his account of the intelligence of laws, but he was never under any illusion as to the practical difficulty of potential movements in that direction, as his attempted analysis of the reasons for the Roman Empire's decline and fall from political hegemony illustrated. Montesquieu was one of the first people to argue cogently that the defeat of the Empire of the Caesars by "barbarian" invasions was not a mere accident of happenstance but an instance of an endlessly repeatable historical pattern, inherent in the logic of empire.

Le Temple de Gnide deals with issues on a much more intimate and personal scale than the *Considerations*, but they are aspects of the same social anthropology, apparently subject to similar repetitions and to the operation of a similar fatality. The most superficial glance at modern fiction, from Nobel prize-winners to TV soap operas, not only reveals the same concerns as Montesquieu's "prose poem" with regard to *gnide,* its rituals and its worship but the same frustrations and the same psychological distress. Superficially, *Le Temple de Gnide* appears to celebrate, or at least to poeticize, *gnide* as a solution to the existential problem of how to discover something worthwhile in human existence, but its underlying rhetoric is profoundly skeptical. It is not unsympathetic to the opinion, frequently to be found in ancient Greek literature, that sexual attraction is a form of madness inherently dangerous to psychological stability and social order, ever likely to unleash Furies. Contemporary literature includes entire genres that assert the opposite vehemently, insisting that love is the answer, or at least part of the answer, to all existential problems, but like *Le Temple de Gnide*, their deeper rhetoric, embodied in their specific illustrations, carries a different implication, representing *gnide* as a principal and primal source of pain and anguish, whose temporary rewards are subject to inevitable processes of decay and destructive transformation. That is why, in spite of its convolutions, its fantasization, its paradoxical qualities and the difficulties of decoding its instruction, *Le Temple de Gnide* has not lost its relevance as a work of art or as analytical social psychology, and why it still fits quite comfortably into the spectrum of the literature of love.

That is not to say that there has not been progress in the literature of love since 1725, at least in matters of narrative strategy and style—but, like all past progress, that seeming advancement has not settled the question of where, exactly, we ought to be going, and how, exactly, we might hope to get there; nor has it even brought us closer to some such settlement. Because of that, the peculiar and slightly primitive nature of the narrative set out in *Le Temple de Gnide* does not undermine its utility, and it can still contribute, in a conscientiously amusing fashion, to our understanding of the matters underlying its carefully-travestied depiction.

This translation was made from the copy of an undated edition of the text printed in Paris that is reproduced on the Bibliothèque Nationale's *gallica* website.

—Brian Stableford, June 2021

THE TEMPLE OF GNIDE

TRANSLATOR'S PREFACE

AN Ambassador of France to the Ottoman Gate, known for his liking for letters, had bought several Greek manuscripts and brought them to France. Some of those manuscripts having fallen into my hands, I found the work that I am giving here in translation among them.

Few Greek authors have reached us, either because they have perished in the ruins of libraries or by virtue of the negligence of the families who possessed them.

From time to time we recover a few pieces of those treasures. Works have even been found in the tombs of their authors, and—which is almost the same thing—this one was found among the books of a Greek bishop. Neither the name of the author nor the era in which he lived is known; all that we can say is that it is not anterior to Sappho, since there is mention of her in the work.

As for my translation, it is faithful; I believed that the beauties that were not in my heart were not beauties, and I have often quit a less vivid expression in order to adopt one that expressed its thought better.

I have been encouraged in this translation by the success obtained by that of Tasso.[1] The person who made it has not thought it bad that I am following the same career as him; he has

---

1 The Italian poet Torquato Tasso (1544-1585) was the author of the epic poem *Gerusalemme liberata* (1591; tr. into French as *La Jérusalem delivrée* and English as *Jerusalem Delivered*) an imitation of French Medieval romances set during the Crusades. It was greatly admired in nineteenth-century France and was widely used as a textbook in schools, thus becoming familiar to all literary men. The reference must be to the 1724 translation by Jean-Baptiste de Mirabaud, which earned the author election to the Académie française.

distinguished it in such a manner as to fear nothing even from those who had given it the most competition.

This little romance is a kind of picture for which the painter has chosen the most agreeable subjects. The public has found cheerful ideas therein, a certain magnificence in the descriptions and naivety in the sentiments. It has an original character that has made critics ask what its model was, which becomes great praise when a work is not to be scorned in other respects.

A few scholars have not recognized what they call "art." It is not, they say, in accordance with the rules. But if the work pleases you, you will see that their heart is not in accordance with the rules.

A man who dabbles in translation does not suffer patiently that his author is not esteemed by others as much as he has done, and I confess that those messieurs have put me in a furious wrath, but I beg them to let the young judge a book which, whatever language it was written in, was certainly made for them. I beg others not to trouble them in their decisions. It is only heads well-curled and well-powdered who will know all the merit of *The Temple de Gnide*.

With regard to the fair sex, to whom I owe the few happy moments I can count in my life, I wish with all my heart that this work might please them. I still adore it, and if it is no longer the object of my occupations, it is of my regrets.

If grave individuals would like a few works less frivolous from me, I am in a position to satisfy them. For thirty years I have been laboring on a work of twelve pages that should contain everything we know about metaphysics, politics and morality, and everything that great authors have forgotten in the volumes that they have given us on those sciences.

FIRST CANTO

VENUS prefers the abode of Gnide to that of Paphos or Amathonte. She does not descend from Olympus without visiting the Gnideans. She has so accustomed that fortunate people to the sight of her that they no longer feel the sacred horror that the presence of a god inspires. Sometimes she covers herself with a cloud, and is recognized by the divine odor that emerges from her hair, perfumed by ambrosia.

The city is in the middle of a region on to which the gods have poured their benefits with full hands; one enjoys a perpetual spring there; the earth, fortunately fertile there, foresees all wishes; the flocks pass by there without number; the winds only seem to reign there in order to spread the spirit of flowers everywhere; birds sing there incessantly, you would think that the bushes are harmonious; streams murmur in the meadows; a mild warmth enables everything to bloom; the air is only respired there with sensuality.

Next to the city is the palace of Venus; Vulcan built its foundations personally; he worked for his unfaithful wife when he wanted to forget the cruel insult that he uttered before the gods.

It would be impossible for me to give an idea of that palace; only the Graces could describe the things of which it is made. Gold, azure, rubies and diamonds shine there everywhere; but I am painting its riches, not its beauties.

Its gardens are enchanted; Flora and Pomona take care of them; their nymphs cultivate them. Fruits are reborn there under the hand that cooks them; the flowers succeed the fruits. When Venus walks there, surrounded by her Gnidiennes, you would think that their playful frolics would destroy those delectable gardens, but by means of a secret virtue, everything is repaired in an instant.

Venus loves to see the naïve dances of the daughters of Gnide; her nymphs mingle with them. The goddess takes part in their games; she strips herself of her majesty; sitting in their midst, she sees joy and innocence reigning over their hearts.

One discovers in the distance a vast grassland enameled with flowers; the shepherd comes to pick them with his shepherdess; but the one she finds is always the most beautiful, and he believes that Flora has made it expressly.

The river-god Céphissus irrigates that grassland and makes a thousand detours there. He stops the fugitive shepherdesses; it is necessary that they give the tender kiss that they have promised.[1]

When the nymphs approach the bank they stop, and its fleeing waves find waves that are no longer fleeing. But when one of them bathes Cephissus is more amorous still; his waters turn

---

1 In Greek mythology the river-god Cephissus was the father of Narcissus.

around her; sometimes he lifts himself up in order better to embrace; he lifts her, he flees, he draws her away. Her timid companions begin to weep, but he sustains her on his waves, and, charged with such a cherished burden, he carries her over the liquid plain; finally, desperate to quit her, he bears her slowly to the bank, and consoles her companions.

Beside the grassland is a myrtle wood, the paths of which make a thousand detours. Lovers come to tell one another their troubles there; Amour, who amuses them, conducts them via paths that are ever more secret.

Not far from there is an ancient and sacred wood where the daylight only enters with difficulty, oaks that seem immortal bear to the skies a head that evades the eyes. One senses a religious fear there; you might think that it was the dwelling of the gods when humans had not yet emerged from the earth.

When one has found the light of day, one climbs a little hill, on which the temple of Venus is situated; the universe has nothing more holy or sacred than that place.

It was in that temple that Venus saw Adonis for the first time; poison ran to the heart of the goddess. "What!" she said. "Shall I love a mortal? Alas, I sense that I adore him. Let no more prayers be addressed to me; there is no longer any god in Gnide but Adonis."

It was to that place that she summoned the Amours when, stung by a reckless challenge, she consulted them. She was in doubt as to whether she should expose herself to the gaze of the Trojan shepherd.[1] She hid her loins beneath her hair; her nymphs perfumed her; she mounted her chariot drawn by swans and arrived in Phrygia. The shepherd was hesitating between Juno and Pallas but he saw her, and his gaze wandered and died. The golden apple fell at the feet of the goddess; he tried to speak, and his disorder decided the issue.

It was into that temple that the young Psyche came with her mother when Amour,

1 Paris, the son of Priam of Troy, in the story in which he is called upon to judge a beauty contest between three goddesses, and awards the prize to Aphrodite/Venus because she offers him Helen of Troy as a bribe.

who was flying around the gilded paneling, was surprised by one of her gazes. He felt then all the gazes that he made others suffer. "It is thus," he said, "that I wound; I cannot sustain my bow or my arrows." He fell upon Psyche's breast. "Ah," he said, "I am beginning to sense that I am the god of pleasures."

When one enters the temple, one senses a secret charm in the heart, which it is impossible to express; the soul is seized by the delights that the gods only feel themselves when they are in the celestial abode.

All that nature has of the cheerful is combined with all that art can imagine of the noblest, and that which is most worthy of the gods.

A hand, doubtless immortal, has ornamented it everywhere with paintings that seem to respire. One sees the birth of Venus there, the rapture of the gods who see her, her embarrassment at finding herself stark naked, and the modesty that is the foremost of the graces.

One sees the amours of Mars and the goddess there. The painter has represented the god on his chariot, proud and even terrible; Renown flies around him; Fear and Death march before his foam-covered chargers; he goes into battle, and thick dust commences to hide him. On another side he is seen lying languidly on a bed of roses; he smiles at Venus; you only recognize him by the few divine features that remain to him. The Pleasures weave garlands, with which they bind the two lovers, their eyes seem confounded; they sigh; and, attentive to one another, they do not look at the Amours who are playing around them.

In a separate apartment the painter has represented the wedding of Venus and Vulcan; the entire celestial court is assembled there. The god appears less somber, but just as pensive, as usual. The goddess gazes at him with a cold expression of common joy; she gives him a hand negligently, which seems to slip away; she retires from him gazes that scarcely carry and turns toward the Graces.

In another painting one sees Juno performing the marriage ceremony. Venus takes the cup in order to swear an eternal fidelity to Vulcan;

the gods smile, and Vulcan listens with pleasure.

On the other side one sees the impatient god drawing his divine spouse away; she puts up so much resistance that one might think that she was the daughter of Ceres whom Pluto wished to ravish, if the eye that sees Venus could ever be mistaken.

Further away one sees him lifting her up in order to carry her to the nuptial bed. The gods follow in a crowd; the goddess struggles and tries to escape the arms that are holding her. Her robe flees her knees, the fabric flies away; but Vulcan repairs that beautiful disorder, more attentive to hiding her than ardent to ravish her.

Finally, one sees him coming to lie on the bed that Hymen has prepared; he closes the curtains on her, and believes that he can hold her there forever. The importunate troop retires; he is charmed to see them draw away. The goddesses play among themselves; but the gods seem sad; and the sadness of Mars has something as somber as black jealousy.

Charmed by the magnificence of her temple, the goddess wanted to establish her worship there herself; she has regulated its ceremonies, instituted its festivals, and she is simultaneously the divinity and the priestess.

The worship that is rendered to her by almost the entire world is more a profanation than a religion. She has temples in which all the daughters of a city prostitute themselves in her honor, and make a dowry of the profit of their devotion. She has some where every married woman goes once in her life to give herself to whoever chooses her and throws the money she has received into the sanctuary. There are others to which courtesans of all countries, more honored than matrons, go to carry their offerings; finally, there are some where the men are eunuchs and dress as women to serve in the sanctuary, consecrating to the goddess the sex that they no longer have and the one that they cannot have.

But she has wanted the people of Gnide to have a purer worship, and to render her honors more worthy of her. Here, the sacrifices are sighs and the offerings a tender heart. Each lover addresses his prayers to his mistress, and Venus receives them for her.

Everywhere that beauty is found it is adored, as Venus herself is adored, for beauty is as divine as she is.

Amorous hearts come into that temple; they go to embrace the altars of Fidelity and Constancy.

Those who are crushed by the rigors of a cruel woman come to sigh there; they feel their torments diminishing; they find flattering hope in their hearts.

The goddess, who has promised to make the happiness of true lovers, always measures them by their pains.

Jealousy is a passion that one can have, but about which one must keep quiet. One adores in secret the caprices of one's mistress, as one adores the decrees of the gods, which become more just when one dares to complain about them.

Put in the rank of divine favors are fire, the transports of amour, and even fury; for the less one is master of one's heart, the more it belongs to the goddess.

Those who have not given their heart are the profane, who cannot enter the temple; they address their prayers to the goddess from afar, and ask her to deliver them from that liberty, which is only an impotence to form desires.

The goddess inspires young women to modesty; that charming quality gives a new price to all the charms that it hides.

But never, in those fortunate places, does anyone blush at a sincere passion, a naïve sentiment or a tender confession.

The heart always fixes for itself the moment at which it ought to surrender, but it is a profanation to surrender itself without love.

Amour is attentive to the felicity of Gnideans; he chooses the arrows with which he wounds them. When he sees an afflicted mistress overwhelmed by the rigors of a lover, he takes an arrow steeped in the waters of the river of forgetfulness. When he sees two lovers commencing to love one another he fires further arrows at them incessantly. When he sees two whose amour is weakening he enables it suddenly to be reborn or to die, for he always spares the last days of a languishing passion. No one passes to disgust before ceasing to love, but greater sweetnesses cause lesser ones to be forgotten.

Amour has removed from his quiver the cruel arrow with which he wounded Phaedre and Ariadne, which, mingling love and hatred, serves to demonstrate his power as lightning serves to make the empire of Jupiter known.

As the god gives the pleasure of loving, Venus combines it with the joy of pleasing.

Young women enter the sanctuary every day in order to say their prayer to Venus. They express sentiments as naïve as the heart that has engendered them. "Queen of Amathonte," one of them said, "my flame for Tirsis is extinct; I don't ask you to return my amour; only make Ixiphile love me."

Another whispered: "Powerful goddess, give me the strength to hide my love for my shepherd for a while, in order to increase the price of the confession I want to make to him."

"Goddess of Cythera," said a third, "I seek solitude; the games of my companions no longer please me; perhaps I'm in love. Oh, if I love someone, it can only be Daphnis."

On feast days, the girls and boys come to recite hymns in honor of Venus; often they sing her glory in singing their amours.

One young Gnidean, holding his mistress by the hand, sung thus: "Amour, when you saw Psyche, you were doubtless wounded by the same arrows with which you have just wounded my heart; your happiness is not different from mine, for you feel my fires, and I sense your pleasures."

I have seen everything that I describe. I went to Gnide, I saw Thémire[1] there and I loved her;

---

1 The Thémire in the story is a shepherdess, but it might not be a pure coincidence that "Thémire" was a conventional salon nickname disguising Marie-Anne de Bourbon, known as Mademoiselle de Clermont, one of Louis XIV's granddaughters. The name was employed by several painters in symbolic images of "Thémire being crowned by the three Graces," one of which was later used as the basis of a decoration of Sèvres porcelain, samples of which still exist. Montesquieu never went to Louis XV's court at Versailles, but it is not inconceivable

I saw her again and I loved her more. I shall remain in Gnide with her all my life, and I will be the happiest of mortals.

We shall go into the temple, and no lover so faithful will ever have entered it; we shall go into the palace of Venus, and I shall believe that it is the palace of Thémire; I shall go into the grassland and pick flowers that I shall put in her bosom. Perhaps I shall be able to lead her into the boscage where so many paths are confounded, and where she has gone astray . . .

Amour, who inspires me, forbids me to reveal his mysteries.

---

that he might have encountered that "Thémire" at a literary salon, some of which were attended, or even hosted, by princesses of the blood. Such salons had been encouraged briefly at Versailles in the 1690s by Mademoiselle de Clermont's aunt, another Marie-Anne de Bourbon, known as the "dowager" Princesse de Conti. Along with Rousseau and Voltaire, Montesquieu was one of the authors associated with the Enlightenment who were guests of another princess of the blood, Louise de Bourbon, Duchesse de Maine, at the Château de Sceaux.

SECOND CANTO

THERE is another sacred place in Gnide, which nymphs inhabit, where the goddess renders her oracles; the earth does not howl under her feet; hair does not stand up on the head; there are no priestesses as there are at Delphi, where Apollo agitates the Pythia, but Venus listens to herself without playing on their hopes or fears.

A coquette from the isle of Crete came to Gnide; she walked surrounded by all the young Gnideans; she smiled at one, whispered to another, leaned her arm on a third and invited two others to follow her. She was beautiful, and artfully adorned; the sound of her voice was as imposing as her eyes. O Heaven, what alarms did she not cause to the true lovers? She presented herself at the oracle as proud as a goddess; but suddenly, we heard a voice emerging from the sanctuary: "Perfidious individual, how dare you bring artifices into the place where I reign with candor? I shall punish you in a cruel manner; I shall take away your charms, but I shall leave your heart as it is. You will appeal to all the men you see, but they will flee you like a plaintive shadow and you shall die crushed by refusal and scorn."

A courtesan of Nocretis came then, brilliant with the spoils of her lovers. "Go away," said the goddess, "you are mistaken if you think that you are making the glory of my empire; your beauty enables it to be seen that there are pleasures, but it does not give them. Your heart is like iron, and even when you see my son, you are unable to love. Go lavish your favors on the cowardly men who request them and who are disgusted by them; go show them charms that are suddenly seen and then lost forever; you are only appropriate to make my power scorned."

Some time afterwards a rich man came who levied the tribute of the King of Lydia. "You are asking me for something," said the goddess, "that I cannot give, although I am the goddess of amour. You buy beautiful women in order to love them, but you do not love them because you buy them; your treasures are not futile; they will serve to make you lose your appetite for all that is charming in nature."

A young man from Doride named Aristeus presented himself then. He had seen the charming Camille in Gnide and was madly in love with her; he felt all the excess of his amour and he had come to ask Venus how he could love her more.

"I know your heart," the goddess said to him; "you know how to love; I have found Camille worthy of you; I could have given her to the greatest king in the world, but kings merit her less than shepherds."

I appeared then with Thémire. The goddess said to me: "There is no mortal in my empire more submissive to me than you, but what do you want me to do? I cannot render you more amorous, nor Thémire more charming."

"Ah," I said to her, "great goddess, I have a thousand favors to ask of you; determine that Thémire only thinks about me; that she only sees me; that she wakes up thinking about me; that she dreads losing me when I am present; that she hopes for me in my absence; that, always charmed by seeing me, she regrets all the moments that she has spent without me."

THIRD CANTO

THERE are two sacred days in Gnide that are renewed every year; women come there from everywhere to compete for the prize for beauty. Shepherdesses are confounded then with the daughters of kings, for only beauty bears the marks of empire. Venus presides in person; she decides without hesitation; she knows very well who the fortunate mortal is whom she has favored the most.

Helen won that prize several times; she triumphed when Theseus had carried her away; she triumphed when she had been abducted by the son of Priam; and she triumphed again when the gods had returned her to Menelaus after ten years of hope. Thus, that prince, in the judgment of Venus herself, found himself as fortunate a husband and Theseus and Paris had been fortunate lovers.

Thirty young women came from Corinth, whose hair fell in large curls over their shoulders. Ten came from Salamis, who had only seen the course of the sun thirteen times. Fifteen came from the isle of Lesbos, and they said to one another: "I feel very emotional; there is nothing as charming as you; if Venus saw you with the same eyes as me, she would crown you in the midst of all the beauties in the world."

Fifty women came from Miletus. Nothing approached the whiteness of their complexion and the regularity of their features; all showed or promised a beautiful body, and the gods who formed them would have made nothing more worthy of them if they had not tried harder to give them perfections than graces.

Twenty women came from the island of Cyprus. "We have spent our youth in the temple of Venus," they said. "We have consecrated our virginity and even our modesty to her;

we do not blush at our charms; our manners, sometimes bold and always free, ought to give us the advantage over a modesty that is incessantly alarming.

I saw the daughters of the superb Lacedaemon; their robes were open at the sides below the belt in the most immodest fashion, and yet they played the prude and sustained that they only violated modesty out of amour for the fatherland.

Sea famous for so many shipwrecks, you are able to conserve precious deposits. You were calm when the ship *Argo* carried the golden fleece over your liquid plain, and when fifty beauties departed from Colchis were confided to you, you curbed yourself beneath them.

I also saw Oriane, similar to the goddesses; all the beauties of Lydia surrounded their queen. She had sent a hundred young women ahead of her who had presented to Venus an offering of two hundred talents. Candaules had come in person, more distinguished by his amour than by the royal purple; he spent his days and nights devouring Oriane's charms with his gaze, his eyes wandered over her beautiful body and never wearied. "Alas," he said, "I am happy, but that is something only known to Venus and me; it would be greater if it gave rise to envy. Beautiful queen, quit those vain ornaments, drop that inopportune clothing; show yourself to the world; release the prize of your beauty and demand altars."[1]

Next to her were twenty Babylonian women; they had crimson robes embroidered with gold; they believed that their luxury augmented their price. Two of them wore, in order to prove their beauty, the riches that it had enabled them to acquire.

Further away I saw a hundred women of Egypt who had black eyes and hair; their husbands were with them and they said: "The law submits us to you in honor of Isis, but your beauty has an empire over us more powerful

---

1 The story of the infatuation of King Candaules of Lydia for his queen and its unfortunate outcome is told by Herodotus, but the queen is unnamed there; some later recyclings of the story called her Nyssia but Montesquieu's choice of Oriane is idiosyncratic.

than the law; we obey you with the same pleasure as when one obeys the gods; we are the most fortunate slaves in the world.

"Duty answers to you for our fidelity; but only amour can promise us yours. Be less sensible to the glory that you acquire in Gnide than to the homages you can find in your own home with a tranquil husband who, while you occupy yourselves with external affairs, must await in the bosom of your family the heart that you bring back to him."

Women came from the powerful city that sends its vessels to the ends of the earth; ornaments fatigued their superb heads; all the continents of the world seemed to have contributed to their adornment.

Ten beauties came from the place where the day commences; they were daughters of Aurora; and in order to see her they got up before her every day. They lamented the Sun, which made their mother disappear; they lamented their mother, who once showed herself to them as to the rest of mortals.

Under a tent I saw the queen of a people of India; she was surrounded by her daughters, who were already hopeful of the charms of their mother; eunuchs served them and their eyes gazed at the ground, for since they had respired the air of Gnide they had sensed their frightful melancholy redoubling.

The women of Cadix, which is at the extremity of the earth,[1] were also competing for the prize. There is no country in the world where a beauty does not receive tributes, but it is only the greatest tributes that can appease the ambition of a beauty.

The daughters of Gnide appeared then: beauties without ornament, they had graces instead of pearls and rubies. Only the presents of Flora could be seen on their heads, but they were more worthy of the embraces of Zephyr. Their robes had no other merit than those of marking as charming figure and having been woven by their own hands.

------

1 This suggests that "Cadix" might be a misprint for Cadiz, the port in the extreme south-west of Spain, but the reference remains enigmatic.

Among all those beauties the young Camille could not be seen; she had said: "I do not want to dispute the prize for beauty, it is sufficient for me that my dear Aristeus finds me beautiful."

Diana rendered those games celebrated by her presence. She had not come to compete for the prize, because goddesses do not compare themselves with mortals. I saw her alone, and she was as beautiful as Venus; I saw her next to Venus, and she was only Diana.

There never was such a great spectacle; the peoples were separated from one another; the eyes wandered from country to country, from the sunset to the dawn; it seemed that Gnide was the whole world

The gods have divided beauty between the nations as nature had divided it between the goddesses. Here one saw the proud beauty of Pallas, there the grandeur and majesty of Juno, further away the simplicity of Diana, the delicacy of Thetis, the charm of the Graces, and sometimes the smile of Venus.

It seemed that every people had a particular manner of expressing its modesty, and that all those women wanted to play with the eyes; for some uncovered the throat and hid their shoulders while others showed the shoulders and covered the throat; those who hid their feet from you repaid you with other charms; and one blushed here at what was called decency there.

The gods are so charmed by Thémire that they never look at her without smiling at their work. Among all the goddesses there is only Venus who sees her with pleasure, and only the gods do not feel a hint of jealousy.

As one picks out a rose in the midst of the flowers born in the grass, one picks out Thémire among so many beauties; they would not have the time to be her rivals; they were defeated before dreading it. As soon as she appeared, Venus only looked at her. She summoned the Graces. "Go and crown her," she said to them; "of all the beauties I see, she is the only one that resembles you."

FOURTH CANTO

WHILE Thémire was occupied with her companions in the worship of the goddess, I went into a solitary wood. I found the tender Aristeus there; we had met on the day when we had gone to consult the oracle; that was enough to engage us in conversation, for Venus puts into the heart, in the presence of an inhabitant of Gnide, the secret charm that two friends find when they sense the dear object if their anxieties in their arms after a long absence.

Delighted with one another, we felt our hearts yielding; it seemed that tender amity had descended from the heavens to place itself in our midst. We told one another a thousand things about our lives. This is approximately what I said:

✳

I was born in Sybaris, where my father Antilochus was a priest of Venus. In that city one does not put any difference between sensualities and needs; all the arts are banished that might trouble tranquil slumber; prizes are given, at public expense, to those who can discover new sensualities; the citizens only remember clowns who have amused them, and have lost the memory of the magistrates who have governed them.

The fertility of the soil, which produces an eternal abundance, is abused there, and the favor shown by the gods to Sybaris only serves to encourage luxury and laxity.

The men are so effeminate that, their adornment is very similar to that of the women; they tint their complexion so well and curl their hair so artfully, spending so much time correcting themselves at the mirror, that it seems that there is only one sex in the city.

60

The women deliver themselves instead of surrendering; every day sees the desires and the hopes of the day finish; no one knows what it is to love and to be loved; people are only occupied with what is falsely called enjoyment.

Favors only have their own reality there, and all those circumstances that accompany them so well—all the trivia that are so highly prized, the engagements that appear ever grander, the little things that are worth so much, everything that prepares a happy moment, so many conquests instead of one, so many enjoyments before the last—are unknown in Sybaris.

Still, if they had the slightest modesty, that feeble image of virtue might please—but no; their eyes are accustomed to seeing everything, and their ears to hearing everything.

Far from the multiplicity of pleasures giving the Sybarites more delicacy, they can no longer distinguish one sentiment from another. They spent their lives in a purely external joy; they only quit one pleasure that displeases them for another that displeases them even more; everything they imagine is a new subject of distaste.

Their souls, incapable of feeling pleasure, seem only to have delicacy for troubles; one citizen was fatigued all night long by a rose folded up in his bed.

Laxity has so enfeebled their bodies that they cannot shift the slightest burdens; they can scarcely sustain themselves on their feet; the softest carriages make them faint; when they are at feasts, their stomachs fail them continually.

They spend their lives lying on sofas, on which they are obliged to repose all day without being fatigued; they are exhausted when they go to languish elsewhere.

Incapable of bearing the weight of weapons, timid before their fellow citizens and cowardly before strangers, they are slaves ready for the first master.

As soon as I could think, I was disgusted by the unfortunate Sybaris. I love virtue, and I have always feared the immortal gods. "No," I said, "I shall not respire this poisoned air any longer; all these slaves of laxity are made to live in their fatherland, and me to quit it."

I went to the temple for the last time, and, approaching the altars at which my father had sacrificed so many times, I said in a loud voice: "Great goddess, I am abandoning your temple but not your worship; in whatever place on earth I might be, I will burn incense for you, but it will be purer than that which is offered to you in Sybaris."

I departed, and I arrived in Crete. That island is full of monuments to the fury of Amour. One can see the brazen bull there, the work of Daedalus intended to deceive or satisfy the aberrations of Pasiphae; the labyrinth, the artifice of which Amour alone can elude; the tomb of Phaedre, who astonished the sun as her mother hand done; and the temple of Ariadne, who, desolate in the desert, abandoned by an ingrate, has not yet repented of having followed him.

One can see the palace of Idomeneus there, whose return was no more fortunate than those of the other Greek captains; for those who escaped the dangers of an angry element found their houses even more deadly. Irritated Venus made them embrace perfidious wives, and they died by the hands they believed to be most dear.

I quit that island, so odious to a goddess who was to make the felicity of my life some day.

I embarked again, and a tempest cast me up on Lesbos. That is another island scantly cherished by Venus; it has removed modesty from the faces of the women, weakness from their bodies and timidity from their souls. Great Venus, let the women of Lesbos burn in a legitimate fire; spare human nature such horror.

Mytilene is the capital of Lesbos; it is the fatherland of the tender Sappho. Immortal as the Muses, that unfortunate woman burns with a fire that cannot be extinguished. Odious to herself, finding her ennuis in her charms, she hates her sex but always seeks it. "How," she says, "can a flame so vain be so cruel? Amour, you are a hundred times more redoubtable when you enjoy yourself than when you are irritated."

Eventually, I quit Lesbos and fate enabled me to find an island even more profane, which was that of Lemnos. Venus has no temple there; the Lemnians never address their prayers to her. "We reject a worship that softens hearts," they said. The goddess has often punished them, but they bear the punishment without expiating their crime, always more impious as they are more afflicted.

I set to sea again, still searching for some land cherished by the gods; the winds carried me to Delos. I stayed on that sacred isle for a few months but, either because the gods sometimes warn us about what is going to happen or because our soul retains of the divinity from which it emanated some faint knowledge of the future, I sensed that my destiny, and even my happiness, was summoning me to another land.

One night when I was in the tranquil state in which the soul, more itself, sees to be liberated from the chain that holds it captive, she appeared to me; I did not know at first whether she was a mortal woman or a goddess. A secret charm was spread throughout her person; she was not as beautiful as Venus but she was delightful, like her; all her features were not regular, but as a whole they enchanted; you did not find there what one admires, but that which provokes; her hair fell negligently over her shoulders but that negligence was fortunate; her figure was charming; she had the aspect that nature alone gives, the secret of which is hidden even from painters.

She saw my astonishment and smiled at it. Gods, what a smile! "I am," she said, in a voice that penetrated the heart, "the second of the Graces; Venus has sent me to make you happy, but it is necessary that you go to worship her in her temple of Gnide."

She fled; my arms followed her, my dream flew away with her; all that remained to me was a mild regret in no longer seeing her, mingled with the pleasure of having seen her.

I therefore quit the isle of Delos; I arrived in Gnide. I can say that at first I respired amour; I felt that I could not express clearly what I felt; I was not yet in love but I was in search of love; my heart was warmed as if in the presence of some divine beauty. I advanced and I saw in the distance young women who were playing in a meadow; I was immediately drawn toward them. "Insensate that I am," I said, "I have, without being amorous, all the aberrations of amour; my heart is already flying toward unknown objects, and those objects cause it anxiety."

I approached; I saw the charming Thémire; doubtless we were made for one another; I only looked at her, and I believe that I would have died of dolor if she had not spared me a few glances. "Great Venus," I cried, "since you are to make me happy, make me so with that shepherdess; I renounce all other beauties; she alone can fulfill your promises and all the prayers that I will ever make."

FIFTH CANTO

I spoke thus about my tender amours to young Aristeus; they made his own sigh. I soothed his heart by begging him to recount them to me. This is what he said to me; I shall not forget anything, for I am inspired by the same divinity who made him speak.

In all this story you will find nothing but the very simple; my adventures are only the sentiments of a tender heart, my pleasures and my pains; and as my love for Camille makes happiness, it also makes the story of my life.

Camille is the daughter of one of the principal inhabitants of Gnide; she is beautiful, she has a physiognomy that will be painted in all hearts; women who make wishes ask the gods for the graces of Camille; men who see her want to see her forever, or fear seeing her again. She has a charming figure and a noble but modest air and sharp eyes ever ready to be tender, features made expressly for one another, and charms invisibly blended for the tyranny of hearts.

Camille does not seek to adorn herself, but she is better adorned than other women.

She has an intelligence that nature almost always refuses to beauties. She lends herself equally to seriousness and enjoyment; if you wish, she will think sensibly; if you wish, she will banter like the Graces.

The more intelligence one has, the more one will find in Camille. She has something so naïve about her that it seems that she only speaks the language of the heart. All that she says and all that she does has the charms of simplicity; you always find yourself a naïve shepherd; graces so light, so fine and so delicate are remarked, but are even better felt.

With all that, Camille loves me; she is delighted when she sees me, she is sorry when I quit her; she makes me promise to return. I always say that I love her, and she believes me; I tell her that I adore her, and she knows it. When I tell her that she makes the felicity of my life, she tells me that I make the happiness of hers; in sum, she loves me so much that she almost makes me believe that I am worthy of her love.

I saw Camille for a month without daring to tell her that I loved her, and almost without daring to tell myself; the more amiable I found her, the less I hoped to be the man who could render her sensible. Camille, your charms touched me, but they only told me that I did not deserve you.

I searched everywhere to forget you; I wanted to efface your adorable image from my heart, that I might be happy. I could not succeed in that; the image has remained there and it will remain there forever.

I said to Camille: "I loved the noise of society, but I seek solitude; I had ambitious views, but I no longer desire anything except your presence; I wanted to wander in remote climes, but my heart is now only a citizen of the places where you respire; all that is not you has vanished from my sight."

When Camille spoke to me about her tenderness, she still had something else to tell me; she thought she had forgotten what she has sworn to me a thousand times. I am so charmed to hear it that I sometimes pretend not to believe her, in order that she will touch my heart again. Soon there reigns between us the sweet silence that is the most tender language of lovers.

When I have been absent from Camille I want to give her an account of what I have seen or heard. "What are you telling me?" she says to me. "Talk to me about our love; or, if you have not thought anything, and have nothing to tell me, cruel man, let me speak."

Sometimes she says to me, while embracing me: "You're sad."

"It's true," I say to her, "but the sadness of lovers is delectable; I feel my tears flowing and I don't know why, for you love me; I have no reason to lament, but I lament; don't extract me from the languor I'm in, let me sigh my pains and pleasures simultaneously. In the transports of amour my soul is too agitated; it is drawn toward its happiness without enjoying it, instead of which I can savor my sadness at present. Don't wipe away my tears; what does it matter if I weep, since I'm happy?"

Sometimes, Camille says to me: "Love me. Yes, I love you, but how do you love me?"

"Alas, I say to her, "I love you as I loved you, for I can only compare the love that I have for you to that which I had for you before."

I hear Camille praised by all those who know her; their praise touches me as if it were personal to me, and I am more flattered by it than she is.

When there is someone with us, she speaks with so much wit that I am delighted by her slightest words, but I love it even more when she does not say anything.

When she speaks amicably to someone, I would like to be the person to whom she is speaking, when I suddenly make the reflection that I would not be loved by her.

Be careful, Camille, of the impostures of lovers; they will tell you that they love you and they will be telling the truth; they will tell you that they love you as much as I do, but I swear by the gods that I love you more.

When I perceive her in the distance, my mind wanders; she approaches and my mind become agitated; I arrive beside her and it seems that my soul is going to quit me, that that soul is Camille's, and that she is going to animate it.

Sometimes, when I want to obtain a favor from her, she refuses it to me, and in an instant she grants me another. It isn't an artifice; combated by her modesty and her amour, she would like to refuse me everything, and she would like to grant me everything.

She says to me: "Isn't it sufficient for you that I love you? What more can you desire than my heart? "

"I desire," I tell her, "that you commit a sin for me that amour causes, and that great amour justifies."

Camille, if I cease one day to love you, may Fate be mistaken and take that day for the last of my life. May she efface the rest of a life that I would find deplorable when I remember the pleasures that I had in loving.

Aristeus sighed and fell silent, and I understood that he had only ceased to talk about Camille in order to think about her.

SIXTH CANTO

WHILE we were talking about our amours we got lost, and after wandering for a long time we came into a large meadow; we were led by a flowery path to the foot of a frightful rock; we saw an obscure lair and went in, thinking that it was the dwelling of some mortal.

O gods! Who would have thought that the place could be so baleful? Scarcely had I set foot in it than my entire body shuddered and my hair stood on end; an invisible hand drew me into that fatal abode; the more my heart was agitated, the more it sought to agitate further.

"Friend," I exclaimed, "let us go further in, even if our troubles are augmented."

I advanced into the place, where the sunlight never entered and the winds never agitated. I saw Jealousy there; her aspect was more somber than terrible; Pallor, Sorrow and Silence surrounded her, and Ennuis were fluttering around her. She breathed over us, she put her hand upon our hearts and struck us on the head; and we no longer saw, or imagined, anything but monsters.

"Come further in, unfortunate mortals," she said to us; "go find a goddess more powerful than me."

We saw a frightful divinity by the light of the flaming tongues of serpents that were hissing on her head; that was a Fury. She detached one of her serpents and threw it at us; I tried to catch it; already, without my having felt it, it had slid into my heart. I stood there for a moment as if stupefied, but as soon as the poison spread in my veins I thought I was in the middle of Hell; my soul caught fire, and in its violence all my body contained pain; I was so agitated that it seemed to me that I was spinning under the whip of the Furies.

Finally, we abandoned ourselves to our transports; we circled that terrible lair a hundred times; we went from Jealousy to Fury and from Fury to Jealousy; we cried "Thémire!" and we cried "Camille!"; if Thémire or Camille had come we would have torn them apart with our own hands.

Finally, we found the light of day; it seemed importunate to us, and we almost regretted the frightful lair when we had quit it; we collapsed with lassitude, and even that repose seemed insupportable to us; our eyes refused us tears and our hearts could no longer form sighs.

I was tranquil for a moment, though; slumber commenced to pour over me its gentle poppies. O gods! Even that slumber became cruel. I saw images there more terrible than pale ghosts; I awoke at every instant to a new infidelity on the part of Thémire; I saw her . . . no, I dare not say it yet, and what I only imagined while awake I found real in the horror of that terrible slumber.

"It will be necessary, then," I said to myself, getting up, "for me to flee darkness and light equally. Thémire, the cruel Thémire, is agitating me like the Furies. Who would have believed that my happiness would be obliterated forever?"

A fit of fury gripped me. "Friend," I cried, "get up! Let us go and exterminate the flocks that are grazing in this meadow; let us pursue those shepherds whose amours are so placid. But no; I can see a temple in the distance, perhaps it's that of Amour; let us go destroy it, let us break his statue and render our fury redoubtable to him."

We ran, and it seemed that the ardor to commit a crime gave us new strength; we traversed woods, fields and fallow land; we did not stop for a moment; a hill rose up in vain, we climbed it and went into the temple; it was consecrated to Bacchus. How great the power of the gods is! Our fury was immediately calmed. We looked at one another, and saw with surprise the disorder we were in.

"Great god," I cried, "I render you my thanks for having soothed my fury and for having spared me a great crime." And, approaching the priestess: "We have loved the god that you serve; he has come to calm the transports by which we were agitated; no sooner had we entered this place than we felt his present favor; we would like to make him a sacrifice; deign to offer it for us, divine priestess. I shall go in search of a victim and I will bring it to his feet."

While the priestess prepared to deliver the mortal blow, Aristeus pronounced these words:

"Divine Bacchus, you love to see joy on the faces of men; our pleasures are worship for you and you can only be adored by the happiest of mortals. Sometimes you lead our reason gently astray, but when some cruel divinity has taken it from us, there is only you who can return it to us. Black Jealousy holds Amour under her slavery, but you take away the empire that she obtains over our hearts and you make her return to her frightful dwelling."

After the sacrifice was made, all the people assembled around us, and I told the priestess how we had been tormented in Jealousy's dwelling. Suddenly, we heard a great noise and a confused mixture of voices and musical instruments. We emerged from the temple and we saw a troop of bacchantes arriving, who were striking the ground with their thyrses, crying "Evohé!" in loud voices.

Old Silenus followed, mounted on his donkey; his head seemed to be seeking the ground, and as soon as he abandoned his body he swayed as if beating time. The troop had faces smeared with lees. Pan appeared then with his flute, and the Satyrs surrounded their king, Joy reigned with disorder; an amiable folly mingled games, mockery, dances and songs together. Finally, I saw Bacchus; he was on his chariot drawn by tigers, such as the Ganges saw him at the end of the universe, bringing joy and victory everywhere.

At his side was the beautiful Ariadne, Princess, you were still mourning the infidelity of Theseus when the god took your crown and placed it in the heavens; he wiped away your tears; if you had not ceased crying you would have rendered a god more unhappy than you, who are only a mortal. He said to you: "Love me; Theseus fled; no longer remember his love, forget even his perfidy, I shall render you immortal in order to love you forever."

I saw Bacchus descend from his chariot; I saw Ariadne descend; he went into the temple. "Amiable god," she cried, "let us stay in this place and sigh over our amours; let us make these mild climes experience an eternal joy; it is near here that the queen of hearts has placed her empire; let the god of joy reign beside her and augment the happiness of these people, who are already so fortunate.

"For myself great god, I already feel that I love you more. What! Will you be able to appear even more amiable to me one day? It is only mortals who can love to excess and love even more; they alone can obtain more than they hope for, and are more limited when they desire than when they enjoy.

"You will have my eternal amour here. In the heavens, one is only occupied with glory; it is only on earth and in rural places that one knows how to love; and while this troop delivers itself to an insensate joy, my joy, my sighs and even my tears will repeat my love to you incessantly."

The god smiled at Ariadne, and he led her into the sanctuary. Joy took possession of our hearts and we felt a divine emotion; seized by the aberrations of Silenus and the transports of the bacchantes, we took up thyrses and we mingled with the dances and the concerts.

SEVENTH CANTO

WE quit the places consecrated to Bacchus, but we soon felt that our troubles had only been suspended. It is true that we did not have the fury that had agitated us, but a somber sadness had gripped our souls and we were devoured by suspicions and anxieties.

It seemed to us that the cruel goddesses had only agitated us in order to make us foresee the misfortunes to which we were destined.

Sometimes we regretted the temple of Bacchus; soon we were drawn toward that of Gnide; we wanted to see Thémire and Camille, the powerful objects of our amour and our jealousy.

But we had none of the sweetness that one is accustomed to feel when, on the point of seeing a person one loves again, the soul is already delighted, and seems to savor in advance all the happiness that is promised to it.

"Perhaps," said Aristeus, "I shall find the shepherd Lycas with Camille; how do I know that he is not talking to her at this moment? O gods, the infidel takes pleasure in listening to him!"

"It was said the other day," I said, "that Thyrsis, who loved Thémire so much, is going to arrive in Gnide; doubtless he loves her still, It will be necessary for me to compete for a heart that I believed to be entirely mine."

"The other day, Lycas told my Camille that I was insane! I was delighted to hear her praised."

"I remember that Thyrsis brought my Thémire fresh flowers. Unfortunate that I am, she put them in her bosom. 'It's a present from Thyrsis,' she said. Oh, I ought to have torn them away and trampled them underfoot."

"It isn't long ago that I went with Camille to make a sacrifice of two turtle-doves to Venus; they got away from me and flew into the air."

"I had written my name with Thémire's on trees; I had written my amours, reading and re-reading them incessantly; one morning I found them effaced."

"Camille, don't drive away an unfortunate who loves you desperately; amour that is irritated can have all the effects of hatred."

"The first Gnidean who looks at my Thémire I shall pursue all the way to the temple, and I shall punish him, even at the feet of Venus."

Meanwhile, we arrived near the sacred altar where the goddess renders her oracles. The people were like the waves of an agitated sea; some were coming to listen, others were going to seek their response.

We entered into the crowd; I lost the fortunate Aristeus; he was already embracing his Camille but I was still searching for Thémire.

I finally found her; I felt my jealousy increase at the sight of her; I felt my initial fury reborn; but she looked at me and I calmed down; it is thus that the gods send the Furies when they emerge from Hell.

"O gods," she said to me, "how many tears you have cost me! Three times the sun has followed its course; I feared that I had lost you forever. That word made me tremble. I have been to consult the oracle; I didn't ask whether you loved me; alas, I only wanted to know whether you were still alive. Venus came to reply to me that you still love me."

"Excuse," I said, "a misfortune that you would hate if your soul were capable of it. The gods, in whose hands I am, can make me lose my reason, but those gods, Thémire, cannot take away my love.

"Cruel Jealousy has agitated me, as in the Tartarus where criminal shades are tormented; I obtained the advantage from it that I have a better sense of the happiness that there is in being loved by you after the frightful situation in which the dread of losing you put me.

"Come with me, then, into this solitary wood; it's necessary that, by means of loving, I expiate the crimes that I have committed. It is a great crime, Thémire, to believe you to be unfaithful."

Never could the woods of Elysium, which the gods have made expressly for the tranquility of shades that they cherish, and never could the forests of Dodona, which speak to humans about their future felicity, nor the gardens of the Hesperides, whose trees are bent over by the weight of the gold that composes their fruits, be more charming than that boscage enchanted by the presence of Thémire.

I remember that a satyr who was following a tearful nymph saw us and stopped. "Fortunate lovers," he cried, "your eyes are able to hear and to respond, your sighs are repaid by sighs; but I spend my life on the track of a grim shepherdess, unhappy while I pursue her and even more unhappy when I have caught her."

A young nymph, alone in the woods, perceived us and sighed. "No," she said, "it is only to augment my torments that cruel Amour makes me see such a tender lover."

We found Apollo sitting next to a spring; he had followed Diana, whom a timid fallow deer had led into the woods. I recognized him by his blond hair and the immortal troop that surrounded him. He tuned his lyre; it attracted the rocks, the trees followed it and the lions were rendered motionless. But we drew further into the forest, summoned in vain by that divine harmony.

Where do you think I found Amour? I found him on the lips of Thémire, and I found him then on her breast; he ran away to her feet, but I found him there again; he hid under her knees, but I followed him, and I would have followed him forever if Thémire, in tears, irritated Thémire, had not stopped me; he was in his last retreat; it is so charming that he was not able to quit it. It is thus that a tender warbler, when dread and amour retains her over her chicks, remains immobile under the avid hand that approaches, and cannot consent to abandon them.

Unfortunate that I am! Thémire listened to my plaints, and was not softened; she heard my pleas and became more severe; finally, I was bold, and she became indignant; I trembled, and she seemed to be annoyed; I wept, she thrust me away; I fell, and I felt that my sighs would have been my last sighs if Thémire had not put her hand on my heart and had not recalled it to life.

"No," she said, "I am not as cruel as you, for I have never wanted to make you die, and you want to draw me into the night of the tomb. Open those dying eyes if you do not want mine to close forever."

She kissed me; I received my forgiveness, alas, without any hope of becoming culpable.

A PARTIAL LIST OF SNUGGLY BOOKS

MAY ARMAND BLANC *The Last Rendezvous*
G. ALBERT AURIER *Elsewhere and Other Stories*
CHARLES BARBARA *My Lunatic Asylum*
S. HENRY BERTHOUD *Misanthropic Tales*
LÉON BLOY *The Tarantulas' Parlor and Other Unkind Tales*
ÉLÉMIR BOURGES *The Twilight of the Gods*
CYRIEL BUYSSE *The Aunts*
JAMES CHAMPAGNE *Harlem Smoke*
FÉLICIEN CHAMPSAUR *The Latin Orgy*
BRENDAN CONNELL *Unofficial History of Pi Wei*
RAFAELA CONTRERAS *The Turquoise Ring and Other Stories*
ADOLFO COUVE *When I Think of My Missing Head*
QUENTIN S. CRISP *Aiaigasa*
LUCIE DELARUE-MARDRUS *The Last Siren and Other Stories*
LADY DILKE *The Outcast Spirit and Other Stories*
ÉDOUARD DUJARDIN *Hauntings*
BERIT ELLINGSEN *Now We Can See the Moon*
ERCKMANN-CHATRIAN *A Malediction*
ALPHONSE ESQUIROS *The Enchanted Castle*
ENRIQUE GÓMEZ CARRILLO *Sentimental Stories*
DELPHI FABRICE *The Red Spider*
BENJAMIN GASTINEAU *The Reign of Satan*
EDMOND AND JULES DE GONCOURT *Manette Salomon*
REMY DE GOURMONT *From a Faraway Land*
REMY DE GOURMONT *Morose Vignettes*
GUIDO GOZZANO *Alcina and Other Stories*
GUSTAVE GUICHES *The Modesty of Sodom*
EDWARD HERON-ALLEN *The Complete Shorter Fiction*
J.-K. HUYSMANS *The Crowds of Lourdes*
COLIN INSOLE *Valerie and Other Stories*
JUSTIN ISIS *Pleasant Tales II*

www.ingramcontent.com/pod-product-compliance
Lightning Source LLC
Chambersburg PA
CBHW050425110726
47899CB00008B/2859